KIDDING AROUND

The Hawaiian Islands

A YOUNG PERSON'S GUIDE

SARAH LOVETT

ILLUSTRATED BY MICHAEL TAYLOR

John Muir Publications
Santa Fe, New Mexico

With Special Thanks
Jacqueline
Tim
Eda
Johnny and Marcy
Zelie Pollon
Todd Bailey
The Ungerleider Family
Jeannie Quinn, Kauai
Tori, Nancy, and Carroll Taylor,
    Oahu
Virginia Fish and Haleakala
    Waldorf School, Maui
Mrs. Claire Rodriguez and her
    5th grade class, Haleakala
    School, Maui
Ms. Eleanor Dudley and her 6th
    grade class, Haleakala
    School, Maui
Mr. Gary McDanniel and his
    4th grade class, Haleakala
    School, Maui
Shereen Waterman and David,
    Hawaii
Will McFarlane
Lisa Freauff and her 4th grade
    class at Island School, Kauai
5th graders at Island School,
    Kauai
Susan Tuttle, Director, Island
    School, Kauai
Al Deloso, Chief of Recreation,
    Maui County Department of
    Parks and Recreation
Louie Silva, State Harbor Divi-
    sion, Marine Patrol, Maui
Kristina Olin, 9
Ron Borkowski, Kona Recrea-
    tion Supervisor, Hawaii
    County Department of
    Parks and Recreation
Laurieanne Chu, Oahu
Mrs. Marcy Frenz and her 6th
    grade class at Mountain View
    Elementary School,
    Mountain View, Hawaii
Lilian Ong, U'ilani Lee, and
    Manu Boyd, Hawaii Visitors
    Bureau
Joseph Ciotti, Aerospace Lab,
    Windward Community
    College, Oahu
Loretta Yajima
Patti Bott and Tobey, 9
And, of course, Al and the gals

John Muir Publications, P.O. Box 613, Santa Fe, NM 87504

© 1990 by Sarah Lovett
Illustrations © 1990 by Michael Taylor
Cover © 1990 by John Muir Publications
All rights reserved. Published 1990
First edition. First printing

Library of Congress Cataloging-in-Publication Data

Lovett, Sarah, 1953-
    Kidding around the Hawaiian Islands: a young person's
guide/
Sarah Lovett; illustrated by Michael Taylor. — 1st ed.
        p. cm.
    Summary: Describes sights and events of interest in
Hawaii, including beaches, caves, and canyons.
    ISBN 0-945465-37-8
    1. Hawaii—Description and travel—1981- —Guide-
books—Juvenile literature. 2. Children—Travel—
Hawaii—Juvenile literature.
[1. Hawaii—Description and travel—Guides.] I. Taylor,
Michael, 1953-   ill. II. Title.
DU622.L68   1990
919.6904'4—dc20   90-5527
                                                          CIP
                                                          AC

Distributed to the book trade by:
W.W. Norton & Company, Inc.
New York, New York

Typeface: Trump Medieval
Typesetter: Copygraphics, Santa Fe, New Mexico
Designer: Joanna V. Hill
Printer: Guynes Printing, Albuquerque, New Mexico
Printed in the United States

Contents

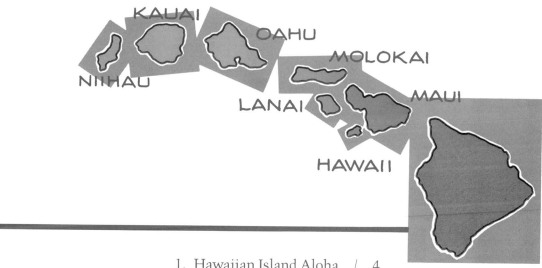

1. Hawaiian Island Aloha

Don't bug me! When the first Marquesans (Poly-nesians) set foot on Hawaii, they were greeted by more than 60 varieties of endemic (native) Hawaiian birds like the nene (Hawaiian goose) and the koloa (Hawaiian duck). What they did not find were frogs, snakes, mosquitoes, fleas, lice, or gnats. So they didn't get bugged. Today, many species of plants and animals have become extinct. Conservation is crucial.

People, brown ones, yellow ones, white ones, pink ones, and black ones, a rainbow of colors, races, and cultures—that's Hawaii. Now add lush rain forests, the world's largest mountain, steaming volcanoes, and postcard perfect beaches—that's Hawaii. Don't forget rare birds like the nene, the unusual wholphin, tiny green geckos, and fabulous puffer fish. All that's Hawaii, too. In fact, this island state is teeming with diversity, whether it's people, geography, or flora and fauna.

There are eight islands in the Hawaiian archipelago, but most tourists visit Oahu, Maui, Hawaii, or Kauai. Scientists believe the islands began to form about 30 million years ago with volcanic eruptions deep in the ocean floor. Lava hardened and built up in layers until the highest mountains in the world were formed. Eventually, the islands evolved into the tropical paradise they are today; each one with its own flavor and style.

Hawaii, the Big Island, has cowboys, active volcanoes, and plenty of room to move at a slow and easy pace.

As Maui, where the demigod Maui lassoed the sun, increases in popularity and population, resorts, hotels, and shopping malls are growing up around its wide, smooth shoreline.

If you've never been to Kauai, the garden isle, you've probably seen its fabulous beaches in the movies.

Oahu, the most visited of all the islands, has everything from traffic jams to the world's best surfing.

Whatever your destination, grab your sunscreen, shades, boogie board, mask, fins, snorkel, raft, camera, and flip flops, and go Hawaii!

Action-Packed Activities
Depending on your schedule and your budget, the islands offer some very special activities. If you're on a limited allowance, you might want to plan ahead and save money for one of the "biggies" listed below.

Hawaii's total land area:
  6,425 square miles
Hawaii's total population:
  approximately 915,000
Hawaii's highest elevation:
  Mauna Kea, 13,796 feet
The wettest spot in Hawaii:
  Mount Waialeale,
  Kauai, with 500 inches
  of rain per year.

Oceangoing raft trips are #1 when it comes to fun, snorkeling, cave dodging, and whale watching. Some companies use avon rafts (like the coast guard), but flat bottom zodiac rafts bump and glide over white-capped waves like wet roller coasters. You might see spinner dolphins, giant manta rays, and even humpback whales (in season). Lunch, snacks, and snorkel equipment are provided on the half-day trips. Captain Zodiac is one company that offers rides from the four main islands.

Helicopter excursions are an exciting way to get a bird's-eye view of steamy, fiery volcanic activity on the Big Island or to whizz down and hover in the great cracks and crevices of beautiful Waimea Canyon on Kauai. Trips are expensive. Ask a travel agent or your hotel about company safety records.

Atlantis Submarine, departing from Waikiki, Oahu, and Kona-Kailua, Hawaii, is the way to get 150 feet underwater without getting wet. You can view multitudes of fish, every color of the rainbow guaranteed, through the thirteen viewing ports. The excursion lasts two hours and costs about $35 for kids 4 to 12 years old and almost twice as much for adults.

For high flying, try **para sailing** on Oahu or Maui. It's great for all ages. At Para Sail Hawaii Inc., you must weigh at least 65 pounds to go up, so if you're feeling like a lightweight, you might ask about sailing with a partner.

A **kayak** excursion on Kauai is a great way to explore the waterfalls, ancient canals, and buffalo herds in Hanalei Wildlife Refuge. A three-hour guided tour costs about $45 per person at Kayak Kauai.

*If you want to impress folks, you'll have to catch a mighty big fish when you're **deep-sea sport-fishing** off the Kona Coast of Hawaii. Pacific blue marlin record-breakers weigh in at well over 1,000 pounds. Other fish include tuna, ono, mahimahi, and shark. But take note: deep-sea fishing is not for the squeamish or faint of heart.*

A dreamy **glider ride** above the green hills and valleys of Kauai is the closest you can get to a trip on a magic carpet. Tradewinds is a locally owned company where you can soar with the best.

Breeze an 18-speed mountain **bike** down a dormant volcanic crater for a windy thrill. It's downhill all the way because a van takes you up to the top of Mauna Kea on Hawaii or Haleakala on Maui. All you have to do is strap on a safety helmet, sunglasses, and elbow pads and start peddling. This is recommended for anyone over ten years old and five feet tall; but no beginners, please. Cost: at least $50. Hawaiian Eyes Big Island Bicycle Tours or Cruiser Bob, with their custom-designed cycles, are two well-known companies.

Snorkel Molokini! This magical reef (just minutes off the coast of Maui) is the place to meet the very best tropical fish, manta rays, eels, and other sea critters. If you're staying on Maui and love to snorkel, this is for you.

Club Lanai is another activity off Maui. Boat over for an all-day adventure of snorkeling, sports, and food. Some kids love it; others think it's too "clubby."

2. Hawaiian Time

KAMEHAMEHA
SHIP

25-40 million years ago volcanic eruptions deep in the ocean floor began to form the mountains of the Hawaiian archipelago.

A.D. 500–800—Seafaring Polynesian natives of the Marquesas Islands in their wooden canoes follow the stars, ocean currents, and winds to the islands of Hawaii.

1100–1300—Voyagers from the Tahitian islands arrive on the islands, now called Hawai'ia, or "burning Hawaii." They conquer the Marquesans and make them slaves or drive them off the islands.

1778—British captain, James Cook, lands on Kauai and names the island chain the Sandwich Islands, after his patron, the Earl of Sandwich.

1779—Captain Cook and a group of his sailors are killed in a confrontation with Hawaiians at Kealakekua Bay on the island of Hawaii.

1780—Each island is ruled by independent chiefs who are born to their position.

1795—Chief Kamehameha of Hawaii (a.k.a. Kamehameha the Great and Kamehameha I) defeats the other chiefs and unites six of eight Hawaiian islands into one kingdom. At the time of his death in 1819, Kamehameha I has established the Kingdom of Hawaii, which survives until 1893.

Early 1800s—The first whaling ships arrive.

1819—King Kamehameha II (Kamehameha the Great's eldest son, Liholiho) abolishes the kapu system. He and Queen Kaahumanu and Queen Keopuolani arrange a public feast where men and women eat together, thus breaking a very conspicuous kapu.

1820—The first American missionaries arrive from New England to preach Christianity to the Hawaiians.

1840—King Kamehameha III (Kauikeaouli) proclaims Hawaii's initial constitution.

1843—Lord George Paulet forces the cession of the Hawaiian Kingdom to Great Britain, but the action is repudiated that same year by Rear Admiral Richard Thomas.

1845—King Kamehameha III and the Legislature move to Honolulu from the capital at Lahaina, Maui.

1848—Under King Kamehameha III, the Great Mahele (land division) introduces the Western idea of private landownership to Hawaiians.

1850—Honolulu becomes Hawaii's official capital.

1800s–1900s—Immigrants come to Hawaii from many countries including China, Korea, Japan, Portugal, Puerto Rico, and the Philippines.

1855–1863—King Kamehameha IV governs Hawaii.

1863–1872—King Kamehameha V, the last of Kamehameha the Great's direct descendants, governs Hawaii.

☆ "STAND FIRM"
"HAWAII for the HAWAIIANS"
– Queen Liliuokalani

1875—King Kalakaua signs a treaty of reciprocity with the United States. The treaty assures Hawaii of a market for its sugar crop, and the United States is guaranteed the exclusive use of Pearl Harbor as a coaling station.

1891—Queen Liliuokalani, the last Hawaiian monarch, begins her short reign.

January 17, 1893—American businessmen, with the support of 160 heavily armed American marines, overthrow the Hawaiian monarchy.

1894—The Provisional Government converts Hawaii into a republic and Sanford Ballard Dole is proclaimed president.

1898—Hawaii is annexed as a Territory by the United States.

1903—James P. Dole (cousin of S. B. Dole) cans his first pineapple and begins to build a great industry.

1927—The first nonstop flight arrives on Hawaii from the mainland.

1931—Radio-telephone service to the mainland is established.

December 7, 1941—The first Japanese bombs fall on Pearl Harbor.

August 21, 1959—Hawaii joins the American Union as the 50th state.

3. Oahu, That's Who!

Today, *Oahu* stands for "the gathering place." What the word *oahu* really meant to early Hawaiians no one knows. But one thing is certain, if you're looking for company, come to Oahu. This island has beaches and palm trees and people; in fact, about 80 percent of all the people who live in Hawaii live on Oahu. Besides doctors, soldiers, musicians, and surfers, there are skyscrapers. And traffic jams. And peaceful coves. In fact, Oahu, the third largest of the Hawaiian islands, has just about anything you might need or want.

The Beach Buzz

Waikiki Beach Center is popular and crowded. Don't get lost in all those people.

Lanikai Beach is a favorite with families. Swim, boogie board, and wind surf.

Kailua Beach Park is fabulous for swimmers and windsurfers. There's also a pretty lagoon to splash in, windsurf lessons and sail board rentals, and plenty of room for picnics. Lifeguard.

Hanauma Bay offers incredible snorkeling, but come early to avoid the crush!

Bellows Beach is located on a military base. It's great for swimming. Open on weekends. Lifeguard.

Halona Blowhole—"Stop, look, and listen!"

Waimanalo Beach Park is a good spot to check for sand crabs. Besides that, it's beautiful.

Hale'iwa Beach Park has green grass, showers, camping facilities, fishing, and picnic areas. It's a good spot for beginning surfers and boogie boarders when the waves are 2 to 5 feet high.

Ala Moana Beach Park is close to Waikiki and very popular with swimmers. You can also try out boogie boards, snorkeling, surfing, and bodysurfing. Lifeguards, showers, and rest rooms.

CAUTION: Even the calmest beach can be dangerous. *Always* swim with a buddy and have adult supervision.

4. Wiki Wiki Fever

*Keiki means child or children in the Hawaiian language. If you want to keiki around Hawaii, there are lots of things to choose from. Each year, Oahu has a **keiki boogie board competition**. Then there's the annual **Queen Liliuokalani Keiki Hula** competition (August). Keep your ears open for the **Honolulu Boys Choir**. Keiki power!*

***Hawaii Visitors Bureau** has lots of information, and they also publish* He Kukini Hawaii, *with a yearly calendar.*

iki wiki means "hurry up"! If you're looking for action, wiki wiki and go Waikiki where people and water both come in waves. Waikiki's a peninsula set apart from the rest of Honolulu by the Ala Wai Canal. High-rise buildings sprout up like metal weeds. Waikiki Beach goes on and on and on, and it's protected by a reef a half-mile offshore. You can boogie board, swim, para sail, or float around on a rubber alligator. Just because there are zillions of people on the beach doesn't mean you should forget about water safety. All those bodies actually make it harder to see if someone needs help. Keep your eyes open and swim with a buddy.

Waikiki has long been a favorite R&R spot for Hawaiian royalty and international jet-setters. These days, there are endless malls, centers, and plazas in Waikiki.

Kalakaua Avenue is the main drag of Waikiki. Sit back and watch the parade—plastic "grass" hula skirts, Krishna devotees in saffron robes and shaved heads, neon palm trees, aloha shirts, and tourists in-the-pink from all over the world.

The **Royal Hawaiian Shopping Center** covers three blocks (and six acres) of Kalakaua Avenue.

*Right next to the Moana (now Moana-Surfrider) Hotel, check out the mighty **Wizard Stones of Waikiki**. Just by sight you'd never guess these four regular-looking rocks possess the magical powers of Tahitian kahunas, or wizards, but that's how the story goes. If you're into magic and mana (spiritual power), take a while to absorb the vibrations, and if you're not, be respectful anyway.*

Besides shopping, daily offerings include lessons in lei-making and quilt-making and coconut frond weaving.

Waikiki hotels are as common as sunburns, but two rate special visits. The **Royal Hawaiian Hotel** (near the Royal Hawaiian Shopping Center) is a sugary pink palace where you can wander under swaying palms and imagine days past. Queens, presidents, sheikhs, princes, and movie stars like Mary Pickford and Douglas Fairbanks have all slept here. Down the beach, the **Moana Hotel** is even older than the pink palace. Long ago, on hot summer nights, aristocrats puffed on their big cigars and sipped rum and pineapple juice over games of backgammon and poker in the Banyan Court.

The U.S. Army Museum of Hawaii at Fort DeRussy, Kalia Road, has heavy-duty tools of destruction on display. Implements from the American Revolution through the Vietnam War are housed inside a humongous bunker with 22-foot walls. This museum is a reminder of Hawaii's history as a strategic military base.

King's Village on Kaiulani Avenue boasts shops, galleries, and free Hawaiian entertainment. You can also buy a ticket that admits you to **King's Village Heritage Theatre**, the **Mission Houses**, **Bishop Museum**, and the **Planetarium**. Transportation is free.

Kapiolani Park is the perfect 220-acre site to fly kites, watch a game of cricket or soccer, picnic, or sneak a snooze. If you hear Hawaiian ballads, salsa songs, or reggae tunes, they might be coming from **Kapiolani Park Bandstand**. The live entertainment is free and fun. If it's December, finish off your day at the bandstand where runners in Honolulu's 26-mile long-distance marathon find their finish line.

Catch the gyrations at the **Kodak Hula Show** (even if it's a bit corny) on Tuesdays, Wednesdays, and Thursdays at 10 a.m. near the **Waikiki Shell** amphitheater in the park.

The Waikiki Aquarium and the Honolulu Zoo are both part of Kapiolani Park. Explore marine ecology, habitats, and life-styles across the street at the **Waikiki Aquarium**. Display tanks offer visitors a mini view of the flora and fauna floating and swimming in the Pacific Ocean. Small sharks share quarters with turkey and puffer fish. Hawaii's rare and endangered monk seals are on view and the "Edge of the Reef" exhibit is a hands-on re-creation of the island's shorelife.

The **Honolulu Zoo** is the only place on Oahu where island kids can hiss and wiggle at a real, live snake. While this zoo isn't one of the world's greatest, they are noted for nifty bird shows and free summer night concerts for the entire family.

There are more animals to see just minutes from the park. Watch chickens walk a tight rope, parrots play poker, and macaws on roller skates, all part of the Trained Bird Show at **Paradise Park** (Manoa Road). On fifteen acres of jungle gardens, you can also pound poi, make leis, and hula 'til you shake apart.

One border of Waikiki, **Diamond Head** (originally called *Le'ahi*, which roughly translates to "forehead of a tuna fish"), is an extinct volcano crater. British sailors renamed the crater when they mistook volcanic calcite crystals, or fool's diamonds, for the real thing. Hike 760 feet to the rim of the seaside peak for a fabulous view of Waikiki and the south coast of Oahu. Wear

*The **Aerospace Lab** (Puohala Elementary School) is the place to learn about astronomy, astronautics, atmospherology, and aeronautics— the four A's of aerospace. There's the Discovery Pad, a hands-on science lab equipped for experiments, as well as an exhibit area and a library. Science buffs will go way out! (235-2631)*

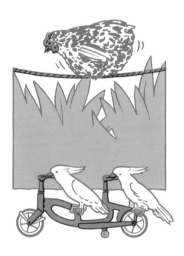

Today **Diamond Head** is a world-famous landmark; long ago it served Hawaiians as the site of the most sacred heiau, or religious temple, on the island. **Papaenaena Heiau** was located below the crater, and the last human sacrifices ordered by Kamehameha the Great took place here following the big Battle of Nuuanu Valley in 1795.

sunscreen and good shoes, and bring a picnic to enjoy near the abandoned gun emplacements, now silent reminders of World War II. A hike up Diamond Head is a local favorite; permits can be obtained in downtown Honolulu at the State Parks Department (1151 Punchbowl St.).

While Waikiki is really a city within a city created for tourists, around it **Honolulu** hums and buzzes like a beehive. It's a center of government, a Pacific port, and the financial hub of the islands. Honolulu can be lots of fun to check out.

As you leave Waikiki and head downtown, stop off at the **Hard Rock Cafe** (Kapiolani and

Kalakaua Ave.) for some loud notes with your burger and fries.

Shop and eat! These are the two main things to do at **Ala Moana Center** (on Ala Moana), one of the world's largest malls. If you can't find the cassette, book, T-shirt, flip flops, or pair of levis you want, maybe a bowl of poi at the mall's giant eating area will restore your shopping mania. Across the street, **Ala Moana Park** is a popular beach recreation area.

Aloha Tower (Pier 9 on the waterfront) used to be the docking point for ocean liners from 1920 to 1950. Even though the ships dock elsewhere these days, it's still a landmark and a great place for a harbor view. Next door at Pier 7, the **Hawai'i Maritime Center's Kalakaua Boathouse** is the perfect haunt for maritime aficionados. Exhibits include ancient Polynesian canoes, windsurf and surf videos, and a replica of a sailor's tattoo parlor. You'll also learn about Duke Kahanamoku, the world's first surf champion.

The ***Falls of Clyde***, also at Pier 7 on the waterfront, is almost a century old. The full-rigged, four-masted ship is the only one of its type left in the world. You can hop aboard, mate, and "Ay ay cap'n!"

Dole Cannery Square (650 Iwilei Rd.) features a multimedia show and a tour of the pineapple cannery where a machine peels and cores 100 pineapples in 60 seconds! You're also encouraged to shop, eat, or visit the **Hawaii Children's Museum of Arts, Culture, Science & Technology**. With six terrific hands-on, minds-on galleries, you might ride bikes with a skeleton to learn about your bones-in-motion, sit on a giant

Ala Wai Harbor is the end of the line for the competitors in the Transpacific Yacht Race from Los Angeles to Honolulu. That's a whopping total of 2,225 miles for the oldest long-distance yacht race in the world. It lasts about one week during June and July of odd-numbered years. Ever since 1906, fans have strolled the marina admiring the sleek and expensive sailcraft as they recover at their moorings.

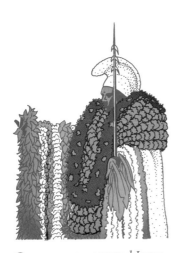

Once a year, around June 11, you'll find 40-foot flower leis decorating **Kamehameha the Great**'s *bronze shoulders (across from Iolani Palace). Kamehameha I is known as the unifier of the islands. He was ambitious, and he was a fierce warrior who led his soldiers in years of battle to defeat rival kings. When he died in May 1819, his bones were hidden away in a sacred place; to this day, they've never been found.*

tongue, examine an insect zoo, or fax your artwork across the museum. If that's not enough, try bubble art and visit **Just For You Kid** toy store and gift shop for special gifts and souvenirs.

A few miles away, on Ward and Beretania in a slightly different part of Honolulu, artists and not-so-artists will enjoy the **Honolulu Academy of Arts** where East and West meet in one of the world's most beautiful museums.

Three 19th-century **Mission Houses** (King St.) present the opportunity to wander through the past. Kitchens, parlors, and bedrooms are all furnished as if the missionaries of old were still in residence. Every Saturday, guides dress up and pretend it's 1831 again.

Across the street, **Iolani Palace** is the only royal palace standing on U.S. soil. It took three years to build and cost about $350,000—a lot of money in 1882. The two royal residents were King Kalakaua and his sister Queen Liliuokalani, who succeeded him to the throne. Later, the deposed queen spent nine months here under palace arrest after American businessmen staged a coup d'etat in 1893. There's a free band concert every Friday noon at the **Bandstand**.

The newest state in the union has a $24.5 million capitol building. **The Hawaii State Capitol** stands next to the palace, and it's built to remind viewers of royal crowns, volcanoes, and palm trees. From February through May, when the State Legislature is in session, you can peer through the big windows off the main courtyard and watch state government in action. Tours can be arranged through the office of the House Sergeant at Arms: 548-7851.

Kawaiahao Church on Punchbowl and King streets contains a series of murals with portraits of the Hawaiian monarchs, their consorts, and all their children. Check it out.

This is a great time to visit **Chinatown**. Chinese, Vietnamese, Hawaiian, Thai, Filipino, Japanese, Korean, and Caucasian folks all live and work side by side in these fifteen blocks.

Take a walk along King Street to Bethel and up N. Beretania to the edge of Aala Park. You can sample duck's feet and dim sum, learn your fortune in a Buddhist Temple, visit an acupuncturist, watch a tattoo artist, or all of the above.

Old Chinatown, 150 years ago, was a rough and rowdy place with cockfights, street brawls, opium dens . . . plenty of action. Saturdays were famous for the aromatic fish market, and young and old alike used to promenade on balmy evenings to see and be seen.

Now Chinatown is cleaner and safer (although Hotel St. is still seedy), but take a grown-up along anyway because they need to have fun, too!

The Chinese Chamber of Commerce offers walking tours on Tuesday mornings. If you can't join them, here are a few highlights.

*Reach out and touch the tactile wall mural at the **Hawaii School for the Deaf and Blind** (3440 Leahi Avenue). Artist Kay Mura and students crafted this work of art for people who can't see. If you can see, close your eyes and imagine another world. Now try to identify some of the many birds, flowers, and fish on the wall.*

Anthony Anjo

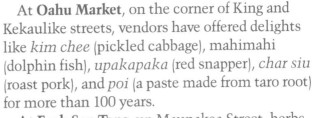

*Toward the end of your wanderings, pop into **Sweetheart's Lei Shop** on N. Beretania. This shop is one of many in the area where you can watch lei-makers as they string blossom after blossom into beautiful and aromatic leis. Pikake and ilima leis make very sweet and special presents.*

At **Oahu Market**, on the corner of King and Kekaulike streets, vendors have offered delights like *kim chee* (pickled cabbage), mahimahi (dolphin fish), *upakapaka* (red snapper), *char siu* (roast pork), and *poi* (a paste made from taro root) for more than 100 years.

At **Fook San Tong**, up Maunakea Street, herbs are king. There are big ones, snake skins, little ones, bone powders, skinny ones, smelly ones, and dried sea horses.

Across the street, **Shung Chong Yuein** has lots of fresh baked goodies like almond cookies, wedding cakes, and moon cakes. After a good walk, these are just desserts.

Wo Fat Restaurant on Hotel and Maunakea is the great-granddaddy of all Honolulu's eateries. More than a century old, it has burned down and been torn down, but it came back each time with more of your favorite Chinese fare.

Take the stage at the old **Hawaii Theatre** on the corner of Bethel and Pauahi streets. Inside, you'll see the frescoes, murals, and columns that represent the Beaux Arts and deco styles of the 1920s and 1930s.

Kuan Yin Temple (N. Vineyard) dates back to the 1880s. There are three altars inside. The center represents Kuan Yin, Goddess of Mercy, on a lotus blossom. The lotus signifies purity. The altar on the right is for Wei Tor, who guards and protects the faith. And on the left altar is Kuan Tai, who stands for justice and truth.

Outside the temple, discover a garden of earthly delights. That's the **Foster Botanic Garden**. It's wonderful, but allow lots of time for all 20 acres.

The **Bishop Museum** on Bernice Street is the

place to explore if you want to learn more about Hawaii's colorful history. Hawaiian Hall is three stories of exhibits that include a thatched Hawaiian house, jewelry made from whale, shark, and dog teeth, weapons, red and yellow feather capes, and a 55-foot sperm whale, a victim of Hawaii's whaling heyday, stuffed and suspended from the roof. On the first Sunday of every month, you'll be admitted free if you bring your parents along. Sit down at the **Planetarium**, next door, and look up at the stars. You might learn the secrets of ancient Polynesian star navigation—how early voyagers sailed 2,400 miles across open sea (without getting lost!) to discover Hawaii.

At 7:55 a.m. on December 7, 1941, the Japanese Air Force flew over **Pearl Harbor** and carried out a strategically brilliant attack that crippled U.S. military forces and caused America to enter into World War II. The assault lasted two hours, damaged 18 vessels, and left 3,000 people dead. The **USS *Arizona***, one of seven battleships anchored in the harbor, sank with 1,100 navy and marine crew on board. That war is over, but all those people are still entombed inside the sunken USS *Arizona*; now it's a memorial to those who died. When you visit the memorial, you have the chance to spend a few minutes reflecting on the ravages of war and the hope for global peace. The names of the dead are inscribed in marble inside. Some people who visit are relatives of those who died. Some cry. Some drop leis into the still waters. (No one under 6 years old allowed.)

Thousands of W.W. II, Korean War, and Vietnam War veterans are buried at **The National**

*Inside the **USS** Bowfin (Halawa Landing next to the **Arizona Memorial Museum**), get the feeling of submersion in an authentic W.W. II submarine. The* Bowfin *has an extensive combat record, but now this sub's in retirement and serves as a museum.*

Hawaii Visitors Bureau

*50,000 people watch the action at **Aloha Stadium**, home of the Hawaiian Islanders Triple-A baseball team. Of course, Wednesdays, Saturdays, and Sundays from 7:30 a.m. to 3 p.m. are the times to swap and shop for local flea market bargains—everything from T-shirts to fish tanks. Call 955-4050 for the Flea Market Shuttle schedule and prices. Across from Aloha Stadium, glide over the ice in the Olympic-size rink of the **Ice Palace**. It's recommended by local kids.*

Nuuanu Pali Lookout is the spot for a fabulous view of the valley. If it's windy (almost always), your hair will stand on end. But don't let story-tellers give you a scare when they tell you Kamehameha the Great sent thousands of Oahuan soldiers over the cliffs to their death in the Battle of Nuuanu, 1795. It's more likely that only a few soldiers fell or jumped to their death.

Memorial Center of the Pacific, in Punchbowl Crater overlooking Pearl Harbor and downtown Honolulu. Punchbowl, *Puowaina*, means "hill of sacrifice."

The beautiful **Nuuanu Valley** is where early *haole* (foreigner) settlers built their homes in Victorian times. It was also the sight of the major Battle of Nuuanu in 1795. A few hours is plenty of time to see highlights in the area.

The **Queen Emma Summer Palace** on Pali Highway is exactly what the name implies. Queen Emma, the wife of Kamehameha IV, stayed here in the summer season. In the queen's master bedroom, look for the royal standards. They have been stripped of their feathers and serve to remind us that on other planes, the soul will be stripped of the body.

Around the corner is **Nuuanu Valley Park** for a moment of peace and reverie among trees and flowers.

Back at Diamond Head, travel away from Waikiki along Oahu's east end to **Hanauma Bay**. This emerald greeny blue bay is a state sealife refuge. The snorkeling is unbelievably perfect, and for that reason, there are lots and lots of people. Come early. That's early! Seven a.m. for starters. You can rent equipment right here.

Turn off at **Halona Blowhole** (peering place) to watch the geyser explode like uncorked champagne.

Sandy Beach and **Makapuu Beach** are known for rowdy and unpredictable surf. Even expert body surfers get into trouble here. It's safest to be a spectator and watch hang gliders leap off inland Makapuu Cliff. Whew! Now, look offshore to the islands. One is slightly bunny

shaped. That's Rabbit Island, a former long-eared hatchery.

Along the **Windward** or **East Shore**, **Kailua Beach Park** (Kalaheo Ave. at Kailua Bay) is a great beach for boogie boarding, windsurfing, and lagoon splashing.

For a quiet moment, stop at the **Byodo-In Temple** (Kaneohe area), a replica of the most gorgeous temple in Kyoto, Japan. The temple and its surrounding classical Japanese garden offer the perfect place to meditate on the beauty of life.

Senator Fong's Plantation & Gardens is the creation of Hawaii's former Senator Fong, the first American of Asian descent elected to the U.S. Senate. A tram will cruise you around the lovely plantation. If you're in the mood for a mellow stop, this might be it.

Past Kaneohe Bay, **Kualoa Regional Park** is a nice picnic and beach area. The Kualoa region

Sea Life Park features the world's only wholphin, a cross between a fake killer whale and a dolphin. Park highlights include the Hawaiian Reef Tank, Ocean Science Theatre, Turtle Lagoon, and Whaler's Cove where porpoises and other sea mammals put on a show!

Monte Costa

Polynesian Cultural Center

*On your way back to Honolulu, the **Dole Pineapple Pavilion** (just north of Wahiawa) boasts delicious frosty Dole Whip cones, fresh fruit, pineapple souvenirs, and a garden filled with many varieties of the famous fruit.*

was sacred to ancient Hawaiians. Today it's known for its great beach and **Kualoa Ranch**, the biggest working cattle ranch on Oahu. Off the park shore, you can't miss **Chinaman's Hat** (Mokoli'i, the Hawaiian name, means "tiny lizard"). At low tide, local families wade out toward this island and poke around the reef. If you decide to follow, wear your tennies.

Past the Crouching Lion Rock Formation, **The Polynesian Cultural Center** (Laie) has 42 acres where you'll see examples of the life-styles of people from Fiji, Hawaii, the Marquesas, New Zealand (Maori), Samoa, Tahiti, and Tonga. Demonstrations include Hawaiian quilt and tapa cloth makers. The Pageant of the Long Canoes is presented in the outdoor theater, and there's a giant buffet and dinner show. Three different ticket packages are available.

Sunset Beach and Oahu's **North Shore** are known for some of the best surfing in the world. At Sunset Point, Gas Chambers, the Banzai Pipeline, Waimea Bay, Himalayas, and Avalanche, watch awesome 25-foot and 30-foot winter waves crash against the beach and make the earth shake. You may be lucky enough to catch a surfing competition in progress when experts take to the tides and risk their boards and even their necks.

At **Waimea Falls Park**, hop aboard the tram or walk to the falls and watch professional divers take the exciting 60-foot plunge.

Haleiwa town is a nice combination of Hawaiians, surfers, and hippies. It's a logical stop for burgers, shave-ice cones, a picnic, and kite flying. **M. Matsumoto Store** (Kamehameha Highway) is especially favored by locals for its shave-ice.

If your idea of fun is a boogie board, a skateboard, or a video game, then only time and technology separate you from ancient Hawaiians. After all, they wanted to have fun, too! And they did — riding holua sleds down slick hillsides, he'e nalu or surfing on handmade giant boards, shooting archery, dancing, putting on puppet shows and plays, and flying kites made of tapa cloth.

5. Big Island Boogie

awaii, the Big Island, boasts the largest active shield volcano in the world! Where else can you stand four feet away from molten lava and see the earth being made?

It's also super for boogie boarding, hiking, swimmming, and snorkeling. One nice thing about Hawaii is that it's BIG. In fact, it's twice the size of all the other Hawaiian islands combined. And the pace of life is slow and easy.

Kamehameha Statue
Pololu Valley Lookout
HAWAI'I
270
250
240
Parker Ranch
19
WAIMEA
Spencer Beach
Hapuna Beach
Waipi'oValley
Anaehoomalu Beach
Mauna Kea
Akaka Falls
HONOMU
19
Hualalai
190
200
Ke ahole Airport
Mauna Loa
Hilo Bay
KAILUA-KONA
HILO
Liliuokalani Gardens
Magic Sand Beach
PPPPELE
Mauna Loa Macadamia Nut Mill
Kahaluu Beach
11
Kealakekua Bay
Kilauea Caldera
Thurston Lava Tube
Lava Tree State Park
PU'UHONUA O HONAUNAU
Place of Refuge
Fern Jungle
PAHOA
Volcanoes National Park
132
11
130
Macadamia Nut Orchards
CHAIN of CRATERS
Kaimu Beach
11
137
KALAPANA
PUNALU'U
Black Sand Beach
Kona Coast
KA LAE (Southpoint)

Hawaii Beach Buzz

Spencer Beach Park It's a terrific place to swim, snorkel, picnic, and camp. The lifeguard is seasonal, handicapped access available, and the white sand plentiful.

Hapuna Beach Park Look for wild kitty cats, picnic facilities, beautiful sand and surf.

Anaehoomalu Bay Windsurfers, this is your beach! There's plenty of shade and the swimming is easy.

Kealakekua Bay If you have a grown-up who's a strong swimmer and the tides are calm, you can swim or snorkel Kealakekua Bay. But remember, there's NO lifeguard and currents can be tricky. On the dry side, poke around the volcanic rocks for tiny crabs or sit in the shade of a tall tree and ponder the 27-foot white obelisk (spire) across the bay. It's a monument to Captain Cook who died here in February 1719.

Kahaluu Beach State Park It is the #1 snorkel beach on the Big Island, and it's also a nature preserve. If you "vant to be alone," don't go in the water. You can be sure lots of sea creatures are cruising along with you. Keep a special eye out for the wonderful green sea turtles who love to visit this bay. Beach rentals are available: masks, fins, snorkels, underwater cameras, flotation vests, and beach chairs.

Magic Sand Beach (a.k.a. White Sands or Disappearing Sands Beach on some maps) is called just plain "Magics" by local beach groupies. It's a great place to boogie board on CALM days. When big waves strike, this beach lives up to its name: the sand disappears like magic. If you're with nonswimmers, there are palm trees to picnic under and volleyball games to watch.

CAUTION: Even the calmest beach can be dangerous. *Always* swim with a buddy and have adult supervision.

6. Don't Pull Pele's Hair!

Kona Side

Kona means south, but the Kona Coast of Hawaii is actually the west and southwest side of the island. With white sand beaches and sunny weather, it's also the side most people visit when they come to the Big Island.

Ke ahole Airport sits somewhere in the middle of the Kona Coast. Highway 19 heads north, and Highway 11 goes south; they both take you to beaches, hotels, and towns.

In the lobby of the **Hyatt Regency Hotel** (on Hwy 19 near Anaeho'omalu Bay), Sarge may greet you from his golden perch. He's a military macaw whose feathers resemble a starched uniform. If you love to be pampered, then the Hyatt might be your cup of posh. Local kids say the swimming pool has a slide that's fun, but you're supposed to be a guest and have a Hyatt beach towel to qualify for splashing.

Farther south, Kailua-Kona is the busiest town on Kona side. **Alii Drive** is the main street in Kailua-Kona if you're looking for beaches, restaurants, and fun things to do. **Kailua Pier**, smack in the center of town, offers you the chance to observe many fishing techniques.

The **Hyatt Regency Hotel** boasts a Dolphin Pond where you can swim with these smart mammals if your name is chosen by lottery. It's expensive, and even though it's exciting to share the water with these amazing relatives, some people think it's not very humane. After all, how would you feel if you were kept inside a small pool where dolphins paid money to swim with you?

Rubber worms, small fish, and assorted snack foods bait the lines. A frequent "catch" is mackerel. Kailua Pier is also a debarkation point for **Captain Zodiac** raft excursions and the **Atlantis Submarine**.

When you walk south along Alii Drive, you'll pass by **Huliheʻe Palace** (now a museum) and under a giant **banyan tree**. Listen to the ear-shattering screech of roosting birds. See if you can spot them in the leafy camouflage, but beware those dreaded droppings.

At **Worldsquare Theatre** in **Kona Marketplace**, you can catch recent flicks and snack on popcorn. One block down and across the street, you'll locate the island's most popular video arcade, the **Fun Factory**. Expect lots of games, no smoke, and adult supervision.

If you're craving outdoor activities but you've had your fill of salt water for the day, stop by **Kona Golf** (on Alii Dr. directly south of the Kona Hilton Hotel) and putt-putt your way through tiny palaces, barns, and along astroturf lanes.

Back on Highway 11, when you're in the mood for Shakespeare or a little theater that's way off Broadway, look for the banner announcing the **Kona Community Players'** latest show. It might be a Neil Simon comedy, *Oliver* (with a kid-studded cast), or Shakespeare's *Midsummer Night's Dream*. There's also a health food store and a tasty café for snacks—anything from chocolate cake, tofu burgers, and turkey sand-wiches to nachos.

Macadamia nuts are one of Hawaii's richest and most delicious crops. **Mrs. Field's Macada-mia Nut Factory** on Highway 11 offers free tours of the selecting, roasting, and toasting. There's free tasting, too.

At the entrance to Anae-hoomalu Bay, you'll dis-cover one of the major groupings of petroglyphs (rock carvings) in the Hawaiian islands. Human "stick" figures and snakelike spirals mark what was the ancient territorial border between Kona and Kohala.

Hawaii Visitors Bureau

Petro-graffiti or graffiti-glyphs? Modern artists like to leave their mark just like their ancient ancestors did. On High-way 19, near Anaehoomalu Bay, white coral messages dot the lava landscape.

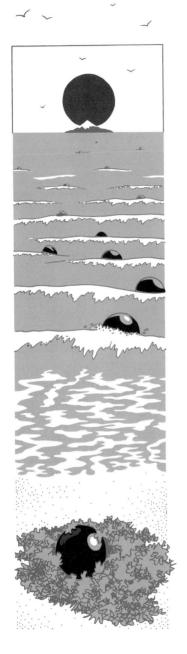

Down the road, at the **Kona Historical Society Museum**, the exhibits are hands-off, but ask to see the video about Kona in the 1930s produced by the seventh graders at Kealakehe Intermediate School. There's also a display of the green glass globes used to buoy fishnets that sometimes float all the way from Japan. You can still find some of these treasures in the waters near Southpoint where it's not too rocky.

Say "giddy-up!" at **King's Trail Rides O'Kona** (by highway marker 111). Saddle up on rental horses and trot along guided trails through forests and fields and overlooking the ocean.

If you take the turn off to Kealakekua Bay, the road winds downhill toward the turquoise bay and the City of Refuge. On the way, you'll pass the **Mauna Kea Royal Kona Coffee Mill**. You're probably not a java drinker, but there are some interesting displays. There's also a glimpse of the noisy mill behind the visitor's shop. Keep your eyes open for an orange and white tabby cat snoozing under coffee beans.

Four miles south of Kealakekua Bay you can take shelter in **Pu'uhonua o Honaunau**, the **Place of Refuge**. Wander among primitive idol carvings, fish ponds, and thatched temples. Ancient Hawaiians had strict *kapu*, or codes of behavior. The word for kapu is *tapu* in Tahitian and *taboo* in English. They all mean the same thing—DON'T!

The *ali'i*, or noble class, were born that way and ruled over the *makaainana* (regular people). The kapu system was created by the ali'i. Some kapu were meant to protect the environment and social structure. Other kapu were really created to benefit a few lucky ali'i. To defy a kapu might mean death by stoning, clubbing, or strangulation. Even walking on a chief's footprints or allowing your shadow to fall on a kapu chief's house could mean curtains. An unfortunate victim served the double purpose of encouraging everyone to play by the rules and of being a sacrifice to a particular god. There was one major bright spot for kapu-breakers: places of refuge were located on different islands, and if a fugitive could escape the chief's warriors, he or she could seek sanctuary in these special shelters.

*****Lyman Mission House
and Museum*** *has a vari-
ety of items on display:
crystals, royal furniture,
rocks that glow in the
dark, and missionary
memorabilia, to name a
few. The old Lyman home
dates back to 1839, and
some local kids say it has
a "ghosty" feel.*

Hilo Side

Hilo is wet, wetter, and wettest. It rains a lot! But
if you don't mind being warm and damp at the
same time, it's a nice town. Hilo has always been
a trading center, from ancient tribal times to more
modern steamship days. It has also been battered by
tsunami (tidal waves), most recently in 1946 and
1960. The oceanfront has been raised and rebuilt
to offer more protection in case of future waves.

Banyan trees canopy all of Banyan Drive where
the big hotels grow. Turn onto Lihiwai Street and
you'll find **Liliuokalani Gardens**, **Coconut Island**,
and **Hilo Bay** right at your fingertips. You should
come equipped with a fishnet, pole, and bucket
because crabbing is legal and fun.

Opposite the gardens, on the bridge to Coconut
Island, cast out your line and then relax under
palm trees with a barbecue cookout.

Where Banyan Drive ends and King Kamehameha Highway begins (a.k.a. Kam Highway),
Ken's House of Pancakes can shake up your Sunday mornings with a game of Scrabble. The
Waiakea Kai Plaza, next door, will fill your stomach and your Saturday night. Whether you chal-
lenge the video games at the **Fun Factory**, catch a
flick at the **Movies-Triplex**, or munch on saimin,
pizza, subs, ice cream, and Bic Macs, it's all one-
stop fun. (Thurs. night is movie dollar night.)

For the sporty, cruise on over to **Hilo Mini Golf**
on Kilauea Avenue and putt-putt past aliens and
automated architecture. You'll need your swim-
suit (nylon works best for a great slick) to slip
down the water slide. After all that exercise,
snack on a Mauna Kea—a snow cone with ice
cream and condensed milk—at the **Mini Shack**.

Mauna Loa Macadamia Nut Mill (5½ miles
south of Hilo) has a mill tour, a chance to view

the nutty assembly line, and a visitor's center for nut purchases.

Continue past the lovely **Nani Mau Gardens** (floral heaven) to **Lava Tree State Park** (in Pahoa) where you can explore the weird sci-fi landscape that's really the result of lava swirling around the tree trunks in its flow-path.

If you keep on heading south, you'll pass black sand beaches like **Kaimu** and **Kalapana**. Black sand is the leftover debris after red-hot lava meets cold ocean water. Kaimu beach is disappearing very slowly over the years. Wear flip flops or shoes because the black sand is hot. Even if the heat tempts you to go in the water, beware the treacherous surf and save swimming for another day.

Ka Lae (**Southpoint**) at the windy southern tip of the island (and the southernmost point of the U.S.) is probably where the first Polynesians landed. If you cruise this way, stop to look for the marks of old canoe moorings in rock. At **Punalu'u** beach, there's a visitor's center and a museum for information about the Ka'u District.

Back in Hilo, travel north on Highway 19, and stop off at the incredible **Hawaii Tropical Botanical Garden**. It's a nature preserve where you'll experience the beauty of a tropical rain forest. See Japanese koi fish at the lily lake, exotic birds, and giant sea turtles. You can move at your own pace on the self-guided tour.

On the way to Akaka Falls, the **Crystal Grotto** in Honomu Village is a local favorite for kids on a budget. Two bits will buy you something nifty, whether you're in the market for tumbled hematite, pyrite, raw crystals, or popcorn rocks that crystallize when you add vinegar.

If you're stir crazy from sitting in a car and you want to get some beans out, the 66 acres of

Don't throw stones at Halema'uma'u Crater! It's Pele's house and the Hawaiian Goddess of Fire should be treated with respect. People who've seen her say she appears in several forms—usually a black-haired young beauty or an old hag— almost always with a little dog at her heels. She can be very courteous, but watch out for her fiery temper; when she's angry, the crater erupts. And if you're tempted to take home a chunk of lava, Pele's "hair" and "tears," think again because Pele's curse means bad luck.

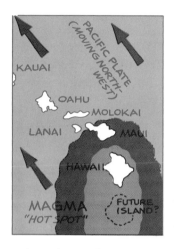

Yikes, the earth is moving! Well, at least the part called the Pacific Plate that runs directly under the Hawaiian islands. This plate (and all the islands with it) is moving northwest at a rate of 5 to 8 centimeters (or 2 to 3 inches) each year. Volcanic vents in the earth's floor remain pretty much where they are. The result is a very slooowwww conveyor belt of islands: each one emerges due south of the one before it. So Kauai is older than Oahu, which is older than Maui. Hawaii, still red-hot today, is the youngest kid on the volcanic block.

Akaka Falls Park is just the ticket. From the parking lot to the falls and back takes about fifteen minutes if you cruise in high gear. Stay on the trails at all times; it's slippery and steep!

The beautiful **Waipi'o Valley** (just north of Honokaa) used to be the center of life on the islands before the Europeans arrived. The swimming pools, 1,300 feet below **Hiilawe Falls**, were filled with fish that Hawaiians could catch with their bare hands. But tsunamis flooded the valley more than once and people moved to safer areas. Today, hiking and four-wheel-drive tours are popular in this valley. **Waipio Valley Shuttle** offers jeep tours, and **Waipio Wagon Tours**—you guessed it.

When you pass through the town of **Waimea**, you can't miss the **Parker Ranch Shopping Center**; it's huge. Nearby Parker Ranch, with 50,000 head of cattle and 224,000 acres, has been called the largest private ranch in America. In the early 1800s, John Palmer Parker offered Kamehameha a deal; he would round up loose and troublesome cattle in exchange for a homestead. He imported Spanish-American cowboys to help with the roping and the branding. The cowboys were (and still are) known as *paniolo*.

A journey to **Volcanoes National Park** is a voyage back to when the earth was steaming, fiery, and barely formed. Hawaii is a "growing baby," and the islands are one of the youngest places on the planet—only about 25 million years old compared to 200 or 300 million years old for the rest of the world's landmass. If you're a sci-fi fan, you'll expect Godzilla or Smog Monster to appear through the eerie gaseous mist. Close your eyes and listen to the hissing explosion as lava rolls into the wild sea. Hawaii's beaches are disappearing and re-forming all the time with new eruptions.

Mauna Kea Observatory *is located on the summit of the "white mountain" that rises 32,000 feet from the ocean floor and counts as the tallest mountain in the world. The University of Hawaii, as well as the U.S. Air Force and NASA, established a major scientific observatory here. France, Great Britain, and Canada have also established their own facilities. Four-wheel tours to the observatory are available, but they're not recommended for kids under 17 because of the dangerous high-altitude conditions.*

Mauna Loa's summit stands 13,677 feet above sea level; it's the largest mountain on earth. More than half of Hawaii's landmass is formed by Mauna Loa, "the whopper" when it comes to the five major volcanoes on the Big Island. It's a "shield volcano" similar in appearance to an upside-down warrior's shield.

Mauna Loa and **Kilauea** are the island's (and the world's) most active volcanoes. Recently, they've been heating things up. Kilauea Caldera erupted about 30 times in a recent two-year period. The giant **Mauna Kea** (with its scientific observatory) and **Hualalai**, also on the Big Island, and **Haleakala**, on Maui, are dormant, but they're not extinct. They could erupt at any time.

Take a hike . . . into **Thurston Lava Tube**. This 15-minute hike is a don't miss. The dark, dank, and drippy tunnel was formed when an outer layer of lava cooled and hardened around a stream of molten lava. Eventually, the red hot stuff flowed right on through, leaving this awesome 450-foot-long, 10- to 20-foot-high tunnel. On your hike, you're surrounded by the fabulous **Fern Jungle**. If you want to spot some native fauna among the flora, keep your eyes peeled for the vermilion and black *'i'iwi* bird and the yellow and olive *amakihi*.

Volcano House hotel (on the rim of Kilauea Crater) is open all year if you want to stay close to the action, but reservations are a must.

When you visit Volcanoes National Park, always make the visitor's center your first stop. They have up-to-the-minute information on fresh lava flows. Stay on marked trails and travel with a buddy. Bring a jacket and wear good shoes. Obey all warning signs and park rangers. Recent lava formations can collapse easily, and fumes are dangerous.

7. Maui for Nowie

aui no ka oi. Maui is the best! That's what Maui's locals and visitors say, and they might be right. The second largest of the Hawaiian islands (728 square miles), Maui was formed from two volcanic peaks. **Haleakala** (House of the Sun), the dormant volcano that forms the eastern end of the island, is only one million years old. On the west end of Maui, you'll discover the beautiful **Iao Valley** and **Puu Kukui**, Hawaii's second rainiest mountain peak (400 inches per year). Of course, Maui's famous beaches are broad and the white sand glistens. Local kids recommend fruit smoothies, boogie boards, dipping in waterfalls on the way to **Hana**, and hiking in **Haleakala Crater**. Whatever you do, don't forget to have a wow of a time on Maui!

*Festivals and parades are part of Hawaii's yearly tradition. **Aloha Week** (Sept./Oct.) and **Kame- hameha Day** are famous for their gigantic parades. **May Day** (Lei Day) on May 1st and the **Merrie Monarch Hula Festival** are two fun and very "Hawaiian" events. The **Annual Ukulele Festival** (ukulele means "jumping flea"), held in July, is the chance to hear energetic Hawaiian tunes.*

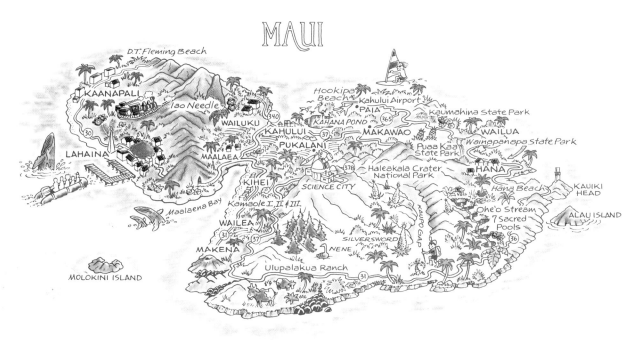

Maui Beach Buzz

Kihei is soft and sandy and good for beginning boogie boarders.

Kamaole I, II, and III are three beach parks in the Kihei area. Kamaole I has showers, rest rooms, and a picnic area. Kamaole III has a playground. The swimming is good, but make sure the lifeguard is on duty because the surf is unpredictable.

Kaanapali Beach is a 2-mile stretch of glistening sand. The swimming is good and the snorkeling is excellent in the

Black Rock area near the Sheraton.

Wailea beaches are tucked in front of big resorts like the Stouffer's Wailea Beach Hotel and the Inter-Continental Maui. These are pretty with good swimming and a gentle drop-off, but make sure you have adults on hand who will keep their eyes on you.

D. T. Fleming Beach Park When the surf is low, this beach is fun for picnics and frisbees. Even though you see people in the

water, heed the signs that warn of dangerous surf.

Hookipa offers an incredible view of some of the world's best windsurfers in action. Championships are held here each year. Waves are big. Professional surfers only!

Hana Beach Park is the safest swimming beach in the Hana area.

Wainapanapa State Park has snorkel spots and a legendary cave.

CAUTION: Even the calmest beach can be dangerous. *Always* swim with a buddy and have adult supervision.

8. Whales and Waves

Most visitors to Maui land at Kahului Airport near the twin cities of **Wailuku** and **Kahului**. Kahului has a deep-water port and **Kahana Pond**, a bird sanctuary where you might spot a few of Hawaii's rare and endangered species. Kahului's main road is bordered by a long row of shopping malls with movies, surf shops, bookstores, and eateries.

Wailuku, the county seat of Maui, governs the islands of Molokai and Lanai as well as Maui. **Kaahumanu Avenue** will lead you to Wailuku's **Main Street**, through town, and onto **Iao Valley Road**. Follow Iao Stream to **Iao Valley State Park** and **Kepaniwai Heritage Gardens**. This pretty park is named after a battle in 1790, when Kamehameha the Great fought against Maui's chieftains. Kamehameha won the fight, but many soldiers on both sides died. *Kepaniwai* means "the damming of the waters" because there were so many dead soldiers in Iao Stream that the water stopped flowing. If you drive on to the end of the road, stop and enjoy the view of the valley and **Iao Needle**, the 2,250-foot cinder cone.

The old whaling port of **Lahaina** is the main hot-spot on Maui. Its small, winding streets are filled with sunburned browsers and shoppers

Many of the big hotels offer luaus. *Pig out on pork, chicken teriyaki, long rice, mahimahi, taro, and poi. After dinner, settle your stomach with a little entertainment.*

Whale Facts. *The biggest dinosaur tipped the scales at 35 tons, but a blue whale can weigh as much as 200 tons. One humpback whale may carry a half ton (yes, folks, that's 500 pounds) of barnacles on its skin. A dolphin has a brain that's 17% larger than a human brain. Each sperm whale tooth weighs more than half a pound.*

from all over the world. Only 200 years ago, Kamehameha the Great, several wives, and three of his children lived in Lahaina. The king's son, Liholiho, ascended to the throne in 1819 as Kamehameha II. Lahaina became the capital of the Hawaiian Kingdom until 1845.

In the early 1800s, ships brought rowdy whalers and pious missionaries to Maui. While the whalers used the port of Lahaina for recreation, the missionaries opened schools for the island's grown-ups and kids. David Malo, a native Hawaiian and a missionary student, grew up to become a famous scholar and philosopher and one of the authors of the first Hawaiian constitution, written in 1840.

The whaling industry lost steam around 1860 when petroleum was discovered on the mainland. These days, whaling in Lahaina means **whale watching**.

What weighs thirty tons, is fifty feet long, breathes air through two blowholes, and commutes by sea from Alaska to Hawaii? If you answered *Megaptera novaeangliae*, you're probably a budding cetologist (scientist who studies whales). The scientific name translates as the "winged New Englander," but the more common name is **humpback whale**.

From December to April each year, Maui is a great spot for whale watching. **Maalaea Bay** is a favorite place for expectant cows (female whales) to deliver their calves (babies). Many boats are available for whale-watch excursions. These mammals can live from 20 to 70 years if they're not slaughtered by commercial whalers. Now, some endangered whales are completely protected, while special limits are imposed for the killing of others. Hopefully, in the near future,

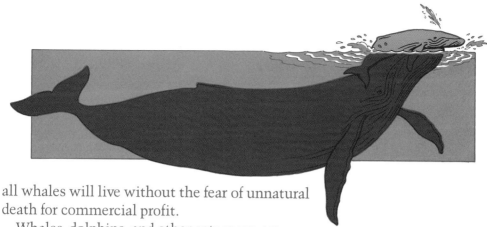

all whales will live without the fear of unnatural death for commercial profit.

Whales, dolphins, and other cetaceans are basically gentle, peaceful creatures. In certain ways, they might be smarter than human beings. **The Pacific Whale Foundation** located in Kihei can give you lots of information about whales and whale watching.

From the Lahaina seawall, look out over the ocean and pick out Lanai and Molokai islands. Now wander along Front Street to the **Hawaii Experience** (824 Front). You might get a bit sea-sick from this 60-foot domed-screen epic, *Islands of the Gods*, but the movie is packed with interesting information and the eight-channel sound system will wake up your ears.

If you happen to be on Front Street on Hallow-een, lucky you! It's a Hawaiian version of Mardi Gras with everything from grass skirts to "Freddy."

When Chinese men were imported to Maui to work in the sugarcane fields, some of them formed a Wo Hing Society chapter of the Chee Kung Tong, a 17th-century Chinese fraternal society. These societies helped maintain a social structure and also functioned as clubs that cared for their aged and infirm members. In 1912, the society built the **Wo Hing Temple** on Front Street which was recently restored. Besides exhibits of

Should we watch whales?
The more we understand about whales, the more we appreciate and care about them. But some cetologists fear that whale watchers may disturb the natural courtship, mating, calving, feeding, and singing habits of whales. Only continued studies will tell how whale watching affects them. In the meantime, boats and people should treat whales with respect and remember two rules: Never get between a whale and her calf; never ride in a boat that chases whales.

*The humongous **banyan tree** in the town square was planted in 1873. This beauty grows over more than two-thirds of an acre and is the biggest banyan in the islands. Sit for a shady while and marvel at the magnitude of this tree towering above your head. Take note: it was only eight feet tall when it was brought from India and planted by Sheriff William O. Smith.*

Chinese history, the **Cook House Theater** runs Thomas Edison movies of Hawaii taken in 1898 and 1903. The **Lahaina Whaling Museum** is chock-full of harpoons, gaffs, navigational instruments, and engraved scrimshaw pieces (whaler's art). It's located in **Crazy Shirts** store and is free.

Farther down Front Street, the **Baldwin Home**, built in 1834, is the oldest standing building in Lahaina. Reverend Dwight Baldwin of Connecticut and his wife sailed to Hawaii in 1830. Baldwin served as pastor of Lahaina's **Old Waine'e Church** for many years. Exploring the house will give you an idea of missionary life, and keep in mind the Baldwins had six children.

Across the street from the square, wander into **The Wharf Cinema Center** for movies, shops, and eats. There's a **Fun Factory** video arcade, as well as frozen yogurt, pizza, subs, and a fish pond filled with giant koi. On the street, pop into the **Pearl Factory** and select an oyster from the bucket. It costs about five dollars, and you're guaranteed a pearl. You don't have to buy anything else.

On the other side of the town square, check out the **Pioneer Inn**, which dates back to 1901 as an inn for seafarers. The walls are covered with whaling memorabilia, photos, and the house rules: "Women is not allow in you room; if you burn you bed you going out; only on Sunday you can sleep all day." You'll also find several restaurants to choose from, including **Haagen-Daz** for a macadamia nut sundae.

Next door, the lawn of the **Public Library** was once a taro patch flooded with water. Farther along the breakwater are the **Hauola Stones**, healing stones used by ancient *kahunas* (powerful healers or spiritual leaders) to cure illness and ease labor pains.

Lahaina Harbor across **Wharf Street** is where you can board the *Carthaginian*. This ship was built in 1920 when it was christened *Mary*, a two-masted schooner. Converted to diesel power and renamed *Komet*, the ship worked as a cement carrier in the Baltic Sea. Now, after a two-year restoration period, the *Carthaginian* is a 93-foot brig (the only authentically restored brig in the world) and a floating museum with a "World of the Whale" exhibition that includes videos of whales.

Recreational activities to choose from in **Lahaina Bay** include sea rafting, wet biking (easier than jet skis), glass bottom boating (on the likes

Teeny weeny, Molokini!
For incredible snorkeling and a fabulous day of underwater fun, take a boat from Lahaina Wharf, Maalaea Harbor, or Kihei Cove to Molokini Crater and dive overboard. This marine preserve is the perfect reef just minutes from Maui's shores. You'll share the seas with a mind-boggling array of fish, manta rays, eels, and even small sharks. Fish even eat from your hands. It's snorkel heaven. While you're in transit, you can fish from equipped boats. One person under 12 recently snagged a 300-pound marlin.

of the Chinese junk, *Lin Wa*), water skiing, windsurfing, and screaming weenie riding.

The **Sugar Cane Train** is a reconstruction of an 1890s narrow gauge. This iron horse chugs six miles through mountains, valleys, and sugarcane fields between Lahaina and Kaanapali. Besides scenic views, you'll learn the history of the sugarcane industry that flourished on Maui in the late 1800s. It's a sedate choo choo.

North from Lahaina, the coast is beautiful, Kaanapali beaches are great, and the **Rainbow Ranch Riding Stables** (near Kapalua) offers sunset rides, pineapple rides, and mountain adventures.

Heading south from Lahaina will take you to **Kihei**. It's several miles long but seems only as wide as a shopping center. Actually, there are lots of malls for stop-and-shop ideas—fast-food, souvenirs, books, kites, and Gecko-Ts. On one side of Kihei you'll find an endless beach where the swimming is good.

At **Kamaole I**, **II**, and **III** beach parks, look for lifeguard stands and posted hours. These beaches are generally safe for beginning boogie boarders.

Even farther south is **Makena Beach**. The sand is great, but waves can be big and unpredictable, so you might want to stay on shore.

Not far from Kihei (at the intersection of Puunene Ave. and Hansen Rd.), stop in at the **Alexander & Baldwin Sugar Museum**. As you explore exhibits like a scale-model sugarcane factory and cockfighting paraphernalia, collect a series of tiny stamps. Each stamp corresponds to a museum display. It's kind of neat.

Haleakala Crater
Maui, a mythical demigod and a magician full of tricks, once lived on the island of the same name.

Paradise Smoothies, *across the street from Kalama Beach Park and McDonald's on S. Kihei Road, is almost always open in case you need a mango, papaya, strawberry, banana, and coconut shake. Don't let the ticky-tack shack fool you. They've been here since 1979. The smoothies, sandwiches, frozen yogurt sundaes, and soups are fabulous. Extras include spirolina, bee pollen, and macadamia nuts, and they're open from 5 a.m. until 2 a.m. (midnight on Sundays)*

According to Polynesian legend, the valley island of Maui used to have very short days and very long nights because the sun was a sleepy head. When the sun finally rose, it would rush across the sky trying to make up for a late start.

Maui's mother, Hina, complained to her son, "I can't dry the kapa cloth I pound from paper mulberry bark because the days are too short!"

Maui knew that the sun first woke up over Haleakala Crater, and he decided to play one of his tricks. That night he wove a rope out of coconut fiber and then he hid behind the edge of the crater. When the sun finally rose, yawning and stretching, Maui lassoed its rays and tied it to the volcano.

Well, the sun begged for mercy and reminded Maui that his mother's cloth would never dry if the sun was dead. So Maui agreed to free the sun; and the sun agreed to go *very* slowly when it

Continued... on next page

crossed the sky above the island of Maui. And that's why Haleakala is such a beautiful place to watch the sun rise.

When you visit the crater be ready for rain, fog, wind, and even snow. You'll travel to a summit elevation of 10,000 feet, and the only thing you can count on is the unexpected.

The view from the summit's Visitor Center in **Haleakala Crater National Park** will knock your socks off. The crater is seven miles long (the entire island of New York City's Manhattan would fit inside) and only 800,000 years old. Haleakala's last eruption was in 1790. It will probably erupt again because it's dormant, not extinct. Hopefully, it won't blow while you're visiting!

At Park Headquarters, say hello to several tame nene. Notice how they've lost most of their foot webbing as they evolved in response to the rough lava.

Those strange shapes on Haleakala's southwest rift are **Science City**, where probes track satellites and beam telecommunications between islands.

Whether you believe in the story of Maui or not, sunrise on the crater is a very spectacular event indeed. The sun comes up like a great orange spaceship and seems to hover directly overhead. Mark Twain (who wrote *The Adventures of Huckleberry Finn*) watched the sunrise in 1873, and he called it "the sublimest spectacle I ever witnessed." You may write your own famous description some day.

On your way up or down, at **Kalahaku Overlook**, check out the awesome five-foot-high silverswords in bloom. If you're a major hiker, you can also take the **Silversword Loop Trail** (0.1 mile), located between Pele's Paint Pot and Holua Cabin.

Stay on the trails: 50 percent of all seedling mortality is due to trampling by careless hiking boots. When these nifty silver plants bloom from June to October, it's a once in a lifetime thing because then they die.

A favorite local hike is a jaunt down **Sliding Sands Trail**. The views are beautiful, and you can turn around whenever you like. For a longer hike, start on Sliding Sands and walk out the Switchbacks, or hike to Holua cabin. Check with the rangers at the Visitor Center for more information. You'll need food, water, warm clothes, energy, and a grown-up.

Bike trips down Haleakala are another local favorite. They're strenuous, and you need to be experienced on a bicycle.

Pony Express Tours offer Haleakala horseback rides. Look for the corral as you drive up the highway to the crater.

Many folks don't consider a visit to Maui complete without an excursion to **Hana**. From Kahului Airport, the drive to Hana (on Hana Highway 36) only takes about four hours, but the road is windy and it's better to give yourself all day for frequent stops. It's possible to count more than 50 bridges on the drive. You can also watch some of the world's best windsurfing, swim in waterfalls, and slurp shave-ice. DO take Dramamine along in case you get a bout of the queasies. You should stay overnight in Hana, but there aren't many places to choose from. One hotel is very expensive, and the less expensive bungalows are usually booked up far in advance. Reservations are necessary.

On the way to Hana, **Paia**, on Highway 36, is a slow and easy "main street" town that looks like

Stay on marked trails!
The environment at Haleakala Crater is very delicate. It varies from arid desert terrain to bogs to rain forests. The natural balance between flora and fauna can easily be disturbed by too many footsteps off the beaten path.

a movie set from the old west. Bakery and café fare includes fruit smoothies, sandwiches, seafood, and chili. On the corner of Baldwin and 36, **Ice, Creams, and Dreams** offers video games, burgers, ice cream, chow fun, and saimin.

Ho'okipa Beach Park is world famous for windsurfing. Top pros come from all around the globe to perfect their style. Several major championships are held here each year. Watch from the cliffs above or venture down to the water's edge, but leave the surfing to the experts. (Take windsurfing lessons or practice your skills in the calmer waters off Lahaina, Kaanapali, and Wailea.)

Kaumahina State Park is a great place to take a break on your trip to Hana. It's an easy walk to Puohokamoa Falls to take a dip and then picnic in the park.

Just past the town of Wailua, swim, splash in the waterfalls, and generally unwind at **Puaa Kaa State Park**.

Waianapanapa State Park is another R&R spot. Seaside, wander through tidepools and caves, hike along the black sand beach, or camp. Waianapanapa has cabins to sleep in. Local kid tips: "It's hot in summer. It rains a lot. Bring mosquito coils. Cabins #4 and #5 are the best."

Hana is a sleepy little town of several hundred folks. Do not, repeat, do not miss the very famous **Hasegawa General Store**. Searching among the many-layered merchandise, you never know what you'll find, and the Hasegawa family is renowned for hospitality all the way from Hana to the mainland. Behind Hana Bay, Ku'uiki Hill was the birthplace of Queen Kaahumanu, King Kamehameha's favorite wife.

Beyond Hana, at **Ohe'o Stream**, **Seven Sacred Pools** flow into each other until they reach the sea. You won't be alone because it's very popular with lots of people and great swimming.

Makawao and **Pukalani** are both Upcountry on Maui. In the early 1800s, King Kamehameha III hired three Mexican cowboys to tame Hawaii's wild cattle. This paniolo tradition lives on in Makawao every July 4th with the rodeo. It's a Maui favorite!

Besides ranching and cowboys, Upcountry Maui is famous for sweet, delicious tomatoes, cucumbers, lettuce, carrots, and Kula onions. During the California Gold Rush, exports from the Upcountry area of Kula fed a lot of hungry '49ers. **Ulupalakua Ranch** has 30,000 acres set aside for agricultural experimentation. Haleakala Ranch was 100 years old in 1989. With 35,000 acres, it's the biggest working cattle ranch on the island.

Beware palm bombs! A palm tree may look shady and inviting when you're spreading out your towel, but bear in mind, those coconuts overhead DO fall off. A direct hit can give you more than a headache!

Aiyah! *(Oh, wow). The Hawaiian language is a snap compared to island pidgin. When early immigrants arrived in Hawaii from places like Portugal, Korea, Japan, and the Philippines, they made up their own common language with a little bit of everything. That's pidgin. Da kine (OK, fine). Hawaiian pidgin changes all the time and it's different on each island. You might* teenk *(think) you're* atsui *(hot stuff), but if you hear local* brohs *(brothers) speaking in a strange tongue, don't expect to understand, but don't discourage communication either. With a little practice, you might be able to make up your own pidgin, or secret language. Ano ai.*

9. Molokai and Lanai—My, My

T he islands of Lanai and Molokai are easily accessible from Maui. Lanai (known as the Pineapple Island) is only seven miles from Kaanapali Beach across AuAu Channel. Besides pineapples and a luxury hotel or two, Lanai offers some of the best snorkeling and diving in the islands. Leeward Lanai beaches are fringed by miles of tropical coral reefs and calm waters where reef fish, Pacific green sea turtles, and spinner dolphins enjoy themselves. From November to May, humpback whales navigate the AuAu Channel to give birth to their calves. Lanai is terrific for snorkel beginners, and catamarans and sailboats depart from Kaanapali Beach, Maui, every morning. Club Lanai is another way to spend a day on this island. Four-wheel vehicles are also available for rent. Lanai highlights include the **Garden of the Gods** rock formation, **Hulopoe** and **Manele Bay**, and **Shipwreck Beach**.

Molokai is "the Friendly Island," but it wasn't always so. In 1866, the Hawaiian monarchy established a colony for sufferers of Hansen's Disease (or leprosy) at **Kalaupapa Peninsula** on Molokai. Seven years later, Father Damien de Veuster, a Belgian priest, came to minister to the

*If you can't go to Kalaupapa, you might want to visit the "old west" town of **Kaunakakai** or **Pukuhiwa Battleground** where four miles of warrior's canoes could be seen at the time Kamehameha the Great tried to unify the islands. It was a major battle, and piles of sling stones are still in the area.*

50

MOLOKAI

Ilio pt.
Pali Coastline
Kepuhi Beach
MAUNA LOA
Mauna Loa
Laao pt.
Hale o Lono Harbor
Palaau State Park
Molokai Airport
46
48
47
KALAUPAPA
Kalaupapa Peninsula
KALAWAO
Kamakou
WAILAU
Moaula Falls
Wailau Trail
Halawa Bay
Cape Halawa
KALANIKAULA Sacred Grove
WAIALUA
KAUNAKAKAI
KAWELA
City of Refuge
Smith~Bronte Landing
July 1927
45
KAMALO
Pukuhiwa Battleground
fishponds

LANAI

Shipwreck Beach
Garden of the Gods
LANAI CITY
Lanaihale
KEOMUKU
Au Au Channel
Keanapapa pt.
Kaumalapau Harbor
Lanai Airport
Manele Bay
Hulopole Bay
KAUNOLU

lepers. At first, he only planned to
stay a few weeks, but instead he spent
the rest of his life on the island helping
the forgotten people until he died of Hansen's
Disease. Modern drugs have been developed to
combat the disease, but some people still chose
to remain at Kalaupapa. Children are not
allowed, so dogs and cats have a very special
place there. Kalaupapa is a National Historical
Park, and access is by air or mule train down a
breathtaking 1,600-foot switchback trail (you
must be at least 16 years old).

Both Lanai and Molokai give visitors a taste of
the earlier years on the islands.

10. Why Kauai?

I t's called "the Garden Isle," and one look will show you why. Kauai is the oldest of the populated Hawaiian islands (remember the Pacific Plate is cruising due northwest?). Ancient stories tell of Hawaiian gods who lived here before humans arrived. Kauai is also the home of the Menehune, a legendary race of minuscule and energetic people reputed to be terrific builders who worked only at night. Myths and stories abound about these magical little people. Some of the caves you'll find on Kauai are said to be their handiwork—and they built them in just one night.

Kauai is shaped almost in a perfect circle. On the South Shore, you can explore the wild Na Pali cliffs and incredible Waimea Canyon. On the North Shore, journey up Wailua River or swim in Hanalei Bay. In any direction, Kauai is filled with natural beauty that's impossible to beat.

Tips from Kauai kids:
Wear shoes when you reef walk; it rains in Kauai, so be prepared to get wet; don't step on centipedes; and don't leave before you try a liliquoi passion fruit.

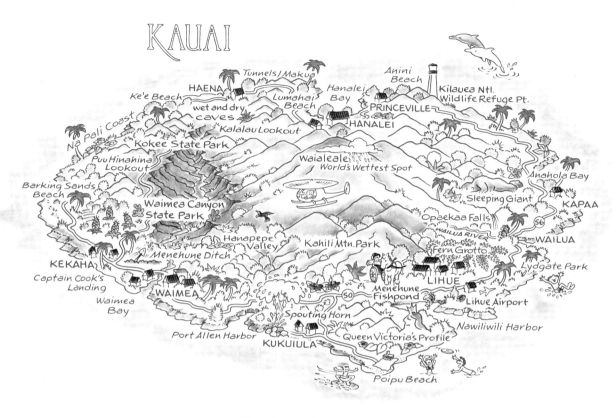

Kauai Beach Buzz

"Tunnels"/Makua is a tricky North Shore beach. Summer is nice for snorkeling. October through May are very dangerous months for surf. Always have an adult with you.

Hanalei Bay is a very beautiful and very dangerous beach. There is surfing, boogie boarding, swimming, and windsurfing. Proceed with caution. Facilities include rest rooms and showers. Hanalei Pier has a daily lifeguard in July and August. The rest of the year, weekends only.

Anini Beach has windsurfing and snorkeling if the surf is gentle. The swimming is nice. Many areas are shallow enough to stand in.

Lydgate Park's protected area is great for younger keiki. Snorkel and feed the fish with peas and carrots from your hand. The unprotected area can be very dangerous. Do not walk on the wall!

Poi'pu Beach is terrific for the whole family. There are plenty of people in this popular park. Look for volleyball games, snorkel, swim, and boogie board. Picnics, too.

CAUTION: Even the calmest beach can be dangerous. *Always* swim with a buddy and have adult supervision.

11. Caves, Kayaks, and Canyons

*Besides boogie boarding, Kauai offers another beach activity—**shell hunting**. Many island beaches are speckled with minute pink and white shells that string into delicate necklaces. See if you can gather a collection of cowry shells or Kahelelani, the itsy bitsy shells that island folks treasure.*

I f you fly to Kauai, you'll land at **Lihue** because it's the only commercial airport on the island. Besides being the seat of county government, Lihue is a nice little town and the departure point for the island's North and South shores. Lihue offers basic eating and shopping (as well as an outdoor laundry mat). Don't miss the **Kauai Museum**. The exhibits include ancient Hawaiian canoes, feather capes, musical instruments, and weapons. Furniture and clothes from the missionary period and more modern times are also on display along with a video of island attractions. The gift shop is a great place to buy unusual cards, toys, and books and souvenirs for yourself.

Heading along the North Shore from Lihue, you'll take Highway 56; Highway 50 follows the coast of the South Shore.

Wailua River Marina is only seven miles from Lihue. From here, depart on ferries to the famous **Fern Grotto**. Smith's river boats are renowned for their on-board entertainment. You might even learn the hula by the time you reach this fern-covered cave.

The 23 acres of **Smith's Tropical Paradise** are filled with gardens, exotic birds, a rain forest, a

Filipino village, and that's just the start. You can take a mini-train or watch an evening spectacular on Kauai's ethnic heritage.

Wailua is the longest navigable river in Hawaii, and it winds through country that was sacred to ancient Hawaiians. Upriver, you'll pass secret burial caves of royalty. To Hawaiians (and other cultures), the bones of their dead are very sacred. In ancient times, they hid them carefully so they would remain undisturbed. The Menehune (some people believe they were the oldest residents of Hawaii) are supposed to have landed at the mouth of Wailua River around A.D. 900.

By road, above the big bend in the river, wander through **Kamokila Hawaiian Village**, a reconstructed native Hawaiian village, and watch traditional craft demonstrations.

Opaekaa Falls plunge 40 feet from a high cliff visible from the road. These "Rolling Shrimp" falls were named for the tiny crustaceans who tumble along its foamy waters.

On the way back to Highway 56, stop a moment at **Poliahu Heiau** and contemplate this site of an ancient temple. Nearby, the **Royal Birthstones** were a favorite place for noble Kauaian women to give birth to royal babies.

Farther up 56, the **Coconut Marketplace** is a notable shopping mall. You might browse at **High As A Kite** for toys and kites or enjoy the free **Children's Hula Show**, Thursday through Saturday at 4 p.m.

Back on the road, keep your eyes peeled for the **Sleeping Giant**. He's only one of Kauai's many peculiar rock formations.

Kilauea National Wildlife Refuge Point is the northernmost point of the main Hawaiian island

*The island of **Niihau** is "the forbidden island." Originally, Pele, the fire goddess, lived here. Later, in 1864, King Kamehameha V sold it to a Scotswoman. Elizabeth Sinclair dedicated Niihau to the preservation of Hawaiian culture, and her descendants still own the island. About 250 pure Hawaiians live there today. No unofficial visitors are allowed.*

chain. It's a pit stop for migrating seabirds and the site of a lighthouse that began flashing its beacon in 1913. The lighthouse was a vital marker (especially for ships bound for Honolulu from the Orient) until it was closed down in 1976. Look for spinner dolphins or humpback whales swimming just one quarter of a mile off-shore. The red-footed boobie and the Laysan albatross are only several species of birds who hang out and fly around here.

Polo fans should make a Sunday picnic and stop at **Anini Beach**, Kalihiwai Bay. That's polo as in ponies and hard-riding gentle men and women.

Speaking of ponies, you can saddle up at **Pooku Stables**, near the Princeville Airport. Riders of all levels are welcome. The country is even more spectacular from a four-footed vantage point.

Princeville Center has restaurants and shops including **Kauai Kite & Hobby Co.** with kites, games, toys, and art supplies.

From the **Hanalei Valley Lookout**, the valley below spreads out like a luscious patchwork quilt made of taro, sugarcane, banana, papaya fields, and a 900-acre National Wildlife Refuge where many endangered island birds find protection. Mount Waialeale, dripping with waterfalls, stands proudly to the south. You'll understand why rainbows are born here.

The horseshoe of **Hanalei Bay** is the place to cool your heels. From the pier you can learn to windsurf and kayak with expert supervision.

56

Local kids whomp around on boogie boards, and the beach is good for snoozing.

In the town of Hanalei, which really winds along the road, keep your eyes open for **Kayak Kauai**. Regular and inflatable rafts are available for rental. Someone wise in the ways of Kauai will guide you along the smooth water of Hanalei River.

For provisions, pull into the **Chin Young Village Center**. Besides the basics—munchies, bamboo fishing poles for about two dollars, pizza, and crab nets—there are tubes, rafts, and bikes to rent at **Pedal & Paddle**. **Jungle Bob's** is the spot for dehydrated carrots, canteens, mosquito repellent, and hiking boots. And **Big Save** has just about anything that's left.

Lumahai Beach is a movie star. This soft and sandy beach is so scrumptious, it has graced postcards, brochures, and home videos all around the world.

Past Haena Point, look inland again for the wet and dry caves. These caverns are nicely creepy, especially the green-slimed wet ones. According to legend, ancient chieftains liked to spend time here. **Maniniholo Dry Cave** is named after the Menehune chief who dug the cave while he was searching for an evil spirit who stole his fish. If you don't believe that story, you might consider that the wet caves, **Waikapalae** and **Waikanaloa**, are the work of Pele, the fiery goddess who was searching for fire. Alas, all she found was the green slime.

Ke'e Beach Park is the end of the line for the North Shore. Enjoy the view of the wild Na Pali Coast, but watch out for tricky surf. If the waves are big, stay out of the water. The trail to the Na Pali cliffs starts here, also. There are hikes for

This is great frog country. While you wander around caves, keep a sharp eye out for "ribets." Another attraction around here are the rivers that lazily cross the road. Cold ponds look great for dipping, but they can be dangerous. Kauai and the other islands have a problem with bacterial contamination from cattle and sheep. If contaminated water gets in your mouth or through skin wounds, it can be fatal.

Captain Cook's Landing marks the spot where the famous British explorer first stepped onto Hawaiian soil in January 1778. The Western explorers, sailors, missionaries, and opportunists who followed in Cook's footsteps changed the course of the islands forever.

those who have a canteen and excess energy. Since the trail is one way, turn around whenever you like. As always, keep a grown-up in tow.

Back in Lihue, if you crave the life of luxury, take an excursion to the **Kauai Westin Hotel**. Besides Clydesdale (beautiful, enormous draft horses) carriage rides, boat rides past small islands dotted with imported wild animals, huge fountains, horseback rides, and endless swimming pools—the list goes on.

Head to the South Shore on 50 past the **Menehune Fish Pond**, which is still used today. In one night, these legendary "little people" built the 900-yard wall to separate the pond from Huleia Stream. It's said the Menehune passed rocks from man to man for 25 miles.

See if you can point to **Queen Victoria's Profile** protruding from the inland mountains.

Turn onto Maluhia Road heading toward the ocean and **Poipu Beach Park**. Poipu means "crashing waves" and this is one of the most popular resort areas on the island. If you get boogie boarded out, watch a game of volleyball in the grassy park, grab a bite of lunch from a snack shop nearby, or fly your kite. This is a wonderful beach for your entire family.

Nearby, on Old Koloa Road and Highway 50, adjacent to **Mustard's Last Stand**, putt-putt through the "tree tunnel," "Waimea Canyon," and "Sleeping Giant" at **Gecko Land Peewee Golf**.

When ocean currents and high tide force waves into a lava tube, the result is the **Spouting Horn**. Ssppllloooossshhhh! A noisy geyser of salty spray will give you a shower if you don't watch out. Local people say the moaning sound comes from the lizard *Lehu*, who crawled inside and got stuck.

Right before the turnoff to Waimea Canyon, there's a short road to **Menehune Ditch**. Those two-foot-high workaholics were at it again. This time they built the ditch for Chief Ola and the local citizens of Waimea who gave them a shrimp feast (their favorite food).

Don't miss a visit to **Waimea Canyon State Park**. This incredible canyon is called the "Grand Canyon of the Pacific" and stretches 14 miles in length and one mile across. When you reach Waimea Canyon Lookout, take your shades off for the 3,400-foot view of the gorge. The colors are mind-blowing—copper, red, orange, gold, green, bronze, blue—and they change with the sun. Look for a rainbow across the canyon rim. If you have any food crumbs, save them for the chickens who cluck cluck near the parking lot.

Puu Hinahina Lookout offers another spectacular view stretching as far as the island of **Niihau**. Even farther up the canyon, **Kokee State Park** is a favorite spot for visitors and locals alike. Who can resist the hiking trails through lush forests and the chance to spy on wild pigs and native birds like the 'i'iwi, 'elepaio, and 'amakihi? Of course, you have to know what they look like first. The **Kokee Natural History Museum**, near the restaurant and the ranger station, is the place to find out about geology, plants, and wildlife in the area. It's also the spot for trail maps.

Rustic cabins are also available for overnights in these mountains. Again, because Kokee State Park is so popular, you must reserve in advance with **Kokee Lodge**.

Kalalau Lookout could take your foggy breath away. It's 4,000 feet to the Kalalau Valley below. Don't get too close to the edge.

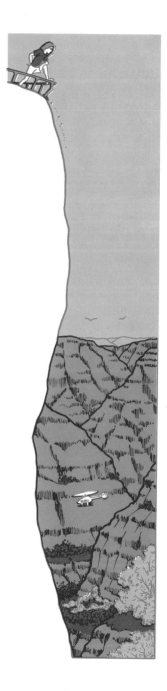

12. Aloha Means Hello, Good-bye

Share your travel discoveries! Send me your tips, recommendations, and gripes, and help keep this book up-to-the-minute: Sarah Lovett, P.O. Box 613, Santa Fe, NM 87504.

Traveling is one of the best ways to become a world citizen. When you experience different lands and people, you grow. When you return home, you take more than souvenirs with you.

Hawaii, with its special beauty and diversity, is a great place to become the ultimate traveler. That means you treat people, animals, fish, and the natural environment with respect. Always leave things as you find them, undisturbed, so the next person can also learn, appreciate, and enjoy. . .just as you have. Because the Hawaiian islands have so many visitors each year, this is especially important.

Ua mau ke ea o ka ʻāina i ka pono. This is Hawaii's state motto. It means, "The life of the land is perpetuated in righteousness." This is good to remember, wherever you are.

When it's time to go, bid the Hawaiian islands "aloha" and remember that means "good-bye," "hello," and "love."

Hawaiian Glossary

Hawaiian	English
aloha	hello, good-bye, love
hale	house
hana	work
haole	foreigner (Caucasian)
heiau	ancient temple
kai	ocean
kamaaina	long-time resident/local
kane	man
kapu	sacred, forbidden
keiki	child
kokua	help
kona	south
mahalo	thanks
makai	toward the sea
malihini	newcomer
mauka	toward the mountains
muumuu	loose dress
ono	delicious
pali	cliff
pau	done, finished
puka	hole
pupu	hors d'oeuvres
wahine	woman
wiki wiki	hurry

The Hawaiian language is the oldest possession of the Hawaiian people. Even though it's very ancient, it wasn't written down until the 1800s when Western missionaries arrived on the islands. The missionaries chose twelve letters for the Hawaiian alphabet; they did this by a popular vote. The consonants they selected are H, K, L, M, N, P, and W. One other consonant is the glottal stop, symbolized by ' and called 'okina in Hawaiian. When you see the ' between two letters, you stop and start again. These days, you'll see the same word used with and without the 'okina. The vowels are the same as those in Western languages. That's why you'll never see a Hawaiian word spelled with an X, F, or B.

Before the missionaries arrived, the Hawaiians shared stories, music, history, and poetry with a rich oral tradition, from mouth to ear. Today, there are about 9,000 native islanders who speak Hawaiian; some of them live on the island of Niihau. Most islanders use Hawaiian words that add a special music to their everyday speech.

Appendix

Aerospace Lab
Puohala Elementary School
45-233 Kulauli St., Rm. A-10
Kaneohe, Hawaii 96744
235-2631

Alexander & Baldwin Sugar Museum
Hansen Rd. & Puunene Ave.
Puunene, Maui
871-8058

Aloha Tower
Honolulu Harbor, Pier 9
Honolulu, Oahu

Arizona Memorial Visitor's Center
Pearl Harbor
Kam Highway, Route 90
Oahu
471-3901/422-2771

Baldwin House Museum
Front St.
Lahaina, Maui
661-3262

Bishop Museum & Planetarium
1355 Kalihi St.
Honolulu, Oahu
847-1443/847-3511

Byodo-In Temple
47-200 Kahekili Hwy.
Windward Oahu

Chinese Chamber of Commerce
42 N. King
Honolulu, Oahu
533-3181

Dole Cannery Square
650 Iwilei Rd.
Honolulu, Oahu
523-DOLE

Falls of Clyde
Honolulu Harbor, Pier 7
Honolulu, Oahu
536-6373

Foster Botanic Garden
180 N. Vineyard Blvd.
Nuuanu, Oahu

Haleakala Crater National park
Haleakala, Maui
Park Headquarters 572-9306/572-9177
Weather information 572-7749

Hawaii Children's Museum
Dole Cannery Square
650 Iwilei Rd.
Honolulu, Oahu
522-0040

Hawaii Maritime Center
Honolulu Harbor, Pier 7
Honolulu, Oahu
523-6151

Hawaii Tropical Botanical Garden
POB 1415
Hilo, HI 96721
964-5233

Hawaii Visitors Bureau
2270 Kalakaua Ave.
Honolulu, HI 96815
923-1811

Honolulu Academy of Arts
900 S. Beretania St.
Honolulu, Oahu
538-3693

Honolulu Zoo
Diamond Head end of Kalakaua Ave.
Kapiolani Park
Honolulu, Oahu

Note: The area code for all Hawaiian islands is 808.

Hulihee Palace
Kailua-Kona, Hawaii

Iolani Palace
S. King St. and Punchbowl St.
Honolulu, Oahu
536-6185 (No kids under 5 yrs.)

Kauai Museum
4428 Rice St.
Lihua, Kauai
245-6931

Kilauea National Wildlife Refuge Point
Kilauea Point Natural History Assoc.
Box 87
Kilauea, Kauai, HI 96754

Kokee Lodge
POB 819
Waimea, Kauai 96796
335-6061

Kokee Natural History Museum
Kokee State Park
335-9975

Kokee State Park
Kauai
Weather information 335-5871

Lyman Mission House and Museum
276 Haili St.
Hilo, Hawaii
935-5021

Mission Houses Museum
553 King St.
Honolulu, Oahu
531-0481

Nani Mau Gardens
421 Makalika St.
Hilo, Hawaii 96720
959-3541

National Memorial Center of the Pacific
Punchbowl Crater
Puowaina Dr., Oahu

Paradise Park
3737 Manoa Rd.
Manoa Valley, Oahu
988-2141

Polynesian Cultural Center
Laie, Oahu's North Shore
293-3333/1-800-367-7060

Pu'uhonua o Honaunau (Place of Refuge)
National Historical Park
POB 129
Honaunau, Kona, HI 96726
328-2326

Queen Emma Summer Palace
2913 Pali Hwy.
Nuuanu Valley, Oahu
595-3167

Sea Life Park
Makapuu Point, Oahu
259-7933

Senator Fong's Plantation
47-285 Pulama Rd.
Kaneohe, Oahu
239-6775/367-4753

State Capitol Building
Capitol Mall
Honolulu, Oahu

U.S. Army Museum of Hawaii
Fort DeRussy, Oahu
543-2639

Volcano House
Volcanoes National Park
Hawaii
967-7321

Volcanoes National Park
Hawaii
Kilauea Visitor Center 967-7311
Eruption reports 967-7977

Waikiki Aquarium
2777 Kalakaua Ave.
Honolulu, Oahu
923-9741

Waimea Falls Park
59-864 Kam Hwy.
Haleiwa, Oahu
638-8511

Kidding Around with John Muir Publications

We are making the world more accessible for young travelers. In your hand you have one of several John Muir Publications guides written and designed especially for kids. We will be *Kidding Around* other cities also. Send us your thoughts, corrections, and suggestions. We also publish other books about travel and other subjects. Let us know if you would like one of our catalogs.

TITLES NOW
AVAILABLE IN THE
SERIES

Kidding Around Atlanta
Kidding Around Boston
Kidding Around the Hawaiian Islands
Kidding Around London
Kidding Around Los Angeles
Kidding Around New York City
Kidding Around San Francisco
Kidding Around Washington, D.C.

COMING SOON

Kidding Around Chicago
Kidding Around the National Parks
  of the Southwest
Kidding Around Philadelphia

John Muir Publications
P.O. Box 613
Santa Fe, New Mexico 87504
(505) 982-4078